I0746002

Rescuing the Rancher

(Christmas Rescue Series)

Cheryl Wright

Copyright

Rescuing the Rancher

(Christmas Rescue Series)

Copyright ©2020 by Cheryl Wright

Small Town Romance Publications

Cover Artist: Black Widow Books

All rights reserved. Without limiting the rights under copyright reserved above, no part of this publication may be reproduced, stored in or introduced into a retrieval system, or transmitted, in any form, or by any means (electronic, mechanical, photocopying, recording, or otherwise) without the prior written permission of the copyright owner of this book.

This is a work of fiction. Characters, places, and incidents are a figment of the author's imagination.

Any resemblance to actual events, locales, organizations or people living or dead, is totally coincidental.

This book was written by a human and not Artificial Intelligence (A.I.).

This book can not be used to train Artificial Intelligence (A.I.).

Dedication

To Margaret Tanner, my very dear friend and fellow author, for her enduring encouragement and friendship.

To Alan, my husband of almost fifty years, who has been a relentless supporter of my writing and dreams for many years.

To You, my wonderful readers, who encourage me to continue writing these stories. It is such a joy knowing so many of you enjoy reading my stories as much as I love writing them for you.

Table of Contents

Chapter One

Mountain Ridge Ranch, Montana

Mid-November 1880

Jonah Saunders stood outside his ranch house sipping coffee. If it wasn't for the overhanging porch he'd be dripping wet by now.

The rain was steady, and he had far too much to do to be standing here wasting time. In a matter of weeks, it would be Christmas. It was hard to believe it was more than a year since he lost his darling Sarah.

He'd been working the ranch that day, and when he came home, she was sitting at the table, face down, not moving. The children were milling around, trying to rouse her. The image would never leave his mind.

The two-year-old twins were crying, running around the room, not knowing what to do. By the time he found her, it was far too late, she'd been long gone. Probably a heart attack, the doc said, but perhaps a clot on the brain.

It was a terrible day, not only for Jonah, but for their children. He worried it would play on their minds as they got older.

Straight away his mother temporarily moved out to the ranch. He walked around in a fog for goodness knows how long. If it wasn't for Ma, he had no idea how he would have managed.

In those first few months she did everything. Bathed, changed, and fed the children, as well as fed the adults. She cleaned the house and did the laundry. She also tried to push him back to reality, to pressure him into being the father he needed to be.

It took time, but he finally got there, but not without the help of Preacher Joseph Dean, who made regular visits to the ranch to check on him.

Ma was not in the best of health, and Jonah determined he needed to make other arrangements. It was her arthritis mostly – as much as she tried, she couldn't do the things she used to do. Even baking was beyond her. As much as he hated the thought, Jonah had to remember his mother was now an old woman.

Ma helped as much as she could, despite his protests, and he truly appreciated it. He just worried for his aging mother. She had spent the best part of adulthood looking after her family on this very ranch, doing far too much despite his father's constant protests. In her earlier days, she had worked as a housemaid.

He spun around as he heard Cora crying. He shoved the door to the ranch open and headed toward the children's room. Leo was still sound asleep, goodness knew how. Cora's high-pitched wailing was enough to wake the devil, as his mother always said.

"There, there, little one," he said lovingly as he picked her up. No doubt she'd been dreaming, or perhaps having a nightmare about that dreaded day when her mother passed. He laid her gently against his shoulder and patted her back to calm her down.

Glancing across at Leo, he noticed the toddler was still sound asleep. If it weren't for his ranch hands, his business would go under, Jonah was certain of it. Things couldn't continue the way they were, with him taking days off to mind the children when his mother wasn't up to it, while his workers took charge of the ranch.

He was beyond grateful for Hank Daley, his foreman. He kept the place together.

Jonah sat Cora on the bed, and glanced down in time to see her flash a smile at him. He gently tickled her tummy and she giggled.

What would he do without his two precious gems to care for? More likely than not he would have totally fallen in a heap and blocked out the entire world.

He was extremely blessed with his two beautiful children, and he knew it. Losing Sarah was the darkest day of his life, and he would never get over it. But he had to press on – had to ensure his off-spring received the love and care they deserved.

Despite all of this, every day was a blessing. Even on the worst days, he still said a prayer of thanks for these two bright sparks in his life.

An idea suddenly flashed in his mind. Perhaps he could advertise for a housekeeper.

Faith Perkins finished polishing the wooden table that sat in the Henrick's kitchen. The house was almost spotless when she arrived and was sparkling by the time she left.

Coming in twice a week seemed pointless, but they insisted. Being the local banker, Mr Henrick insisted the place was perfect in case he decided to hold a dinner party.

He never did.

Mrs Henrick was more than capable of looking after the house herself, but she was certain it was more about appearances than the actual work she performed. If she hadn't needed the small stipend she received from this job, she'd quit in a heartbeat.

She gave the table one last glance, then washed her hands. It was time to prepare biscuits for supper. The stew had been cooking for most of the day and would be ready when Mr Henrick arrived home.

Tomorrow she would clean for the Harrigan's, then the Sanderson's the next day, and two days after that, she'd be back here again. Her own home would be cleaned in between. There was never a day of rest for Faith.

She stretched herself out. She might only be twenty-six but this was hard work. Her body was already complaining, and she was eager to find something that would not be so harsh. Preferably with the one family, perhaps even live in.

Yes, that would work far better, but impossible to find, let alone secure.

Once she arrived home, it started all over again. With her own mother gone, it was left to Faith to look after her father and older brother, drunkards the pair of them, and cook all their meals, not to mention keep house and wait on them hand and foot.

Father took all but two dollars of her weekly earnings, so she was left with virtually nothing to show for her hard work.

She rubbed her neck then turned to the stove, stirring the stew once more before placing the biscuits in the oven.

As she closed the oven door, Faith heard the front door open. "It's only me, Faith," Mr Henrick called as he always did. He was a good employer and never wanted her to get a fright at his sudden arrival.

"Good evening, Mr Henrick," she said brightly. "The biscuits are in the oven, and the stew is ready to serve. Mrs Henrick had a headache and is lying down."

He pulled a face. Faith wished she could lay down sometime. She barely had enough time to sleep at night.

Mr Henrick pulled a newspaper out from under his arm and placed it on the polished table. "I've finished with this," he said. "Do me a favor and place it in the fire on your way out."

"Of course, Mr Henrick," she said, wanting to tell him to do it himself. Why did everyone treat her like a slave?

She snatched the paper up and glanced at the pages Mr Henrick had been reading. One advertisement caught her attention immediately.

Full-time Housekeeper Needed – cooking skills necessary.

It sounded perfect for her. She almost ran into the sitting room and ripped out the page, shoving it into her skirt pocket. She then tore up the remainder of the newspaper and threw the remaining pages into the burning fire.

She would read the entire advertisement when she got home, but it did sound promising. Faith pulled her cloak around herself and mounting the buggy, headed home. Excitement threatened to overwhelm her. But what would her father say?

That was a problem for another time.

As she strolled through the door to her son's house, Martha handed Jonah the mail. Disappointment filled him.

It had been two weeks since he'd placed the advertisement. He was certain the applications would be overwhelming.

Not that he was keen to replace his dear wife, Sarah. He simply had no choice. He needed to have his children cared for, food cooked, and his home kept clean and tidy. There was no other option.

"There are two letters for you," she said, handing the unsealed envelopes over. "The first one reeks of perfume," she said raising her eyebrows. "Did you request a mail order bride or a housekeeper?"

She laughed, but Jonah found none of it funny. This was a last resort, and they both knew it. He scowled at his mother. He'd rather not do this at all. "You open them," he said. "Now that you're here, I need to get to work."

"Really, Jonah. It's your advertisement," she said with exasperation clearly in her voice.

He was at the end of his tether. He'd had to take on extra ranch hands to cover his share of the work and look after his children instead. Not that he begrudged doing it, but he wasn't good at it. Not really.

He glanced up at her as he spooned oats into his young son's mouth.

"He can do that himself you know," she told him scathingly, as she did most mornings. He ignored her words.

Reading his mood, Ma ripped the first envelope open. She glanced at him and rolled her eyes. "I told you this was a bad idea. Mary Adams is a widow with five children. Says she is more than capable of doing the job and would become your bride in a heartbeat."

"Oh for goodness sakes – I didn't advertise for a bride, only a housekeeper! Toss it in the fire, Ma."

He watched the paper burn to a crisp before offering another spoon of oats to Leo.

"This one might be alright," Ma said, her eyebrows raised. "She is a young woman of twenty-six and is currently working as a housekeeper and cook to four different households."

He glanced up at her. "That sounds more like it. But why is she applying if she already has work?"

"Says she needs more stability and is growing tired of going to several houses over the week."

He nodded. "That sounds feasible. Can you write and invite her here for dinner or something? So I can meet her."

"You can write to her yourself. Did you mention the children in your advertisement?" Martha wanted to know. He squirmed in his chair as she scrutinized him closely. "Jonah? Tell me you did."

He continued to squirm. "I thought it might put someone off," he said, glancing across at her while continuing to feed the toddler.

"Seriously, Jonah! You need to tell her when you correspond back." She near-threw the short-handwritten letter at him and left the room as Cora began to wail.

She was right. He knew she was right, but he was getting desperate. It would put any housekeeper off to know she had to care for two young children as well as keep house *and* cook for not only the family, but the ranch hands.

To that end, he included only the bare minimum of information. Besides, it would have cost a packet to include everything in the advertisement.

He decided to write to Miss Faith Perkins himself when he returned from work that evening. His mother would post the letter tomorrow before she returned to the ranch.

Pleased she had called into the Mercantile on her way home, Faith had read and re-read the response she'd received.

Dear Miss Perkins,

Thank you for your application. You sound exactly what I need. I know you live a few hours away in Hallowed Springs, but I would like to meet with you to discuss the position. There is more to it than only housecleaning and cooking, so if you're still interested, please write back to make arrangements.

Kindest regards,

Jonah Saunders

Her heart fluttered – he was interested! Faith didn't dare mention the newsletter advertisement to her father, and carefully folded the letter and placed it in the pocket of her skirt. It was the one place she knew he dare not look.

The last thing he would want would be for Faith to leave home. If she did get the job advertised, she would have to find accommodation at Mountain Ridge, which was another twenty minutes further on than the Mountain Ridge Ranch. It was not much further than she was traveling now, and would be perfect.

This needed to be kept secret or she would never get away. She would have to carefully plan her escape, because it would indeed be an escape for her.

She closed her eyes and prayed it would all work out – she couldn't take much more. She was already on the verge of a break-down.

Sitting at her dressing table in her nightgown, Faith brushed her long brown hair, fifty strokes every night. That's what her mother taught her, and she would continue to do so, even if it was tiresome at times.

She glanced up at the mirror and squinted. The old dresser had outlived its time. The paint was peeling, and one leg had broken, causing it to sit at a slant. If father didn't take her money, what amounted to stealing, she would replace it.

She pondered her difficult situation.

She had to get away. She absolutely must. If this position didn't work out, she'd have to look for something else. There was no other option.

Living ten miles out of Hallowed Springs had its advantages. For one she didn't have to face the locals very often. Besides, they all knew what her father was like. They'd encountered him over the years, and had only tolerated him for her sake.

Faith went straight from home to her cleaning job each day. She avoided all contact with people except the Mercantile.

She had no choice but to go there for supplies. Mrs Stanton was rather strange, but her husband was far easier to deal with.

Of course, she went to church each week. Even when Mother was alive, her father and brother refused to attend church, and she had no intention of pushing them. It was one of the few times she got to spend time away from them, except when she was working.

Besides, they were usually nursing a hang-over on Sunday mornings.

Harry could be downright savage at times. Not that he'd ever laid a hand on her, but there had been times she was convinced he would. Her brother Martin was little better. Had she been born a male, her life would be very different.

When she finished brushing her hair, Faith read over her shopping list. She would drop it at the Mercantile on her way to the Henrick's in the morning. As was her usual routine, she would collect the order on her way home.

She could have it delivered, and was sorely tempted to do so, but the twenty-cent delivery fee came out of her own pocket. Father refused to have it added to his account. Anger flared though Faith. She really needed to leave. Not just from her current work commitments, but from her so-called family.

She prayed the housekeeping job she had applied for would work out. All she had now was hope.

Faith lay down in bed after saying her evening prayers, which always included the wish for a better life. She was on the brink of sleep when her bedroom door flew open. She sprung up in bed with fright.

"What, what's wrong?" she asked in her half-asleep stupor, scurrying further back on the bed.

Harry stood staring down at her, his face contorted in anger, then reached out and snatched her out of bed. "Where's my coffee," he screamed in a drunken stupor. "You forgot my coffee! Get out there and make it," he screamed again, this time so close to her face she could smell the alcohol on his breath and feel the coldness of his heart.

Faith quickly jumped out of bed, and snatching up her robe, ran ahead of him. She hadn't forgotten his coffee – she wouldn't be so stupid as to give him leave to berate her as he'd done. He was almost rolling down drunk, he was so intoxicated.

It made her sick to her stomach.

This was not the first time this had happened, nor would it be the last. At least not unless Faith could put some sort of plan in to place to get away permanently.

She pulled her robe up around herself and bare-footed, headed toward the kitchen. In his drunken stupor, Harry fell sideways, knocking her into the doorway. Faith would be lucky if she didn't have a black eye tomorrow.

His soiled mug was sitting on the kitchen counter – proof she'd provided his evening coffee, but Faith was not stupid enough to tell him so.

He'd once threatened to backhand her for talking back, as he'd called it, and she wasn't willing to tempt fate.

She made his coffee and delivered it to her drunken father in the sitting room. By this time, he was fast asleep in his chair. Martin was passed out in front of the fire.

Disgusting, the pair of them. How had she managed to end up with a lazy good-for-nothing father, and a brother who was no better?

After her mother had died, father began drinking. Only a little at first, but it increased as the years went by. Once Martin was old enough, he was introduced to the same lifestyle her father enjoyed. She would not continue to be a slave to these men who called themselves her family.

Faith vowed to put an end to it any way she could.

Chapter Two

Faith packed up her meagre belongings and placed them under the seat of the buggy. Harry and Martin were still sound asleep after their night of bingeing on alcohol.

They would have an almighty hangover this morning, Faith decided. It was exactly what they deserved.

She was up as normal at daybreak and began preparing supper for her family. She stoked the fire, lit the wood fire stove, and filled the kettle.

She made breakfast and boiled the kettle ready for their morning beverages. The whole time her heart pounded in her ears, terrified they would learn her secret.

The bitterness in her heart awakened as the day progressed. She had worked her fingers to the bone all her adult life. Father and Martin worked at the local timber mill. At least she thought they did, until she ran into the owner recently and found out the pair had been sacked some months ago.

No wonder her father was stealing her wages – he had no money of his own. Bile rose in her throat and she fought it back. How did she not realize she was being cheated by her own father? She felt sick to her stomach and had to go outside for some fresh air.

It wasn't long before Harry and Martin stumbled into the kitchen waiting for their breakfast to be served up to them. It was difficult, but she didn't once deviate from her normal routine in case they got suspicious.

She washed the dishes and tidied the kitchen as normal, then the pair left, supposedly for work, but Faith knew better. Probably going to spend the day at the local hotel, she thought bitterly.

A short time later Faith climbed up onto the buggy she used each day to get to work and pulled her thick coat up around her shoulders. She flicked the reins and was soon on her way.

The ride to Mountain Ridge Ranch would take at least three hours, possibly more depending on the terrain. She would have to go via the outskirts of town to ensure she wasn't seen by Harry, and that would add time to her trip.

As she wound her way through the unknown territory, a shiver ran through her. Once Harry and Martin realized she was gone, there would be an explosion from the pair. But that wouldn't be until after supper when she didn't appear at her usual time.

She could see it now. Harry would be tearing her room to shreds trying to work out where she was. Faith's heart pounded and her hand suddenly reached into the pocket of her skirt. She sighed with relief when she found the advertisement still there.

Faith slowed the buggy as she came to the entrance of Mountain Ridge Ranch, the sign over the gravel road telling her she'd arrived.

She stared down the long drive. Was that the ranch house up ahead? It looked so tiny in the distance, but was no doubt large. She was beyond exhausted – it took far longer to get there than she'd anticipated.

What if they turned her away? After all, they had no idea she was coming.

Faith fought back tears. This was a fool's errand. She should have waited for a response, then planned her escape after that.

But she knew she couldn't. Father had become far too aggressive of late. What if he had harmed her more last night than he already did? He was a big man, and incredibly strong from working at the timber mill all these years. She couldn't risk it.

She lifted the reins and urged the horse forward. Her heart pounding, Faith made her way toward what she hoped would be her new employer.

"Did you hear that?" Martha turned her head toward the front door. "Someone is coming."

Jonah frowned at his mother. "I'm sure you're imagining things. Who would be visiting without notice?"

Cora lay across his shoulder, her favorite place to be, on the verge of sleep. It was time for the children's afternoon nap, and for the adults to eat now that the children had been fed.

Jonah's head shot up at the sound of gravel grating under the wheels of a buggy or wagon. "You're right. Someone is here," he said, walking toward the front door. He opened the door before their visitor had a chance to knock and stood there staring.

A young woman stood before him. The large bruise covering almost half her face made him cringe. She stood on his porch and stared at him in a trance-like state.

"Are you Mr Saunders," she finally asked, her voice low as though she was scared to talk too loudly.

She looked on the verge of collapse, and he ushered her inside. "That's me, Jonah Saunders. Please, come in and sit down," he said warily, leading her to a chair.

His mother reached for Cora, and he gladly handed her over, more concerned with his wary visitor. "I'll put the children to bed," she said. "It is already past their nap time."

As she continued toward the chair, the woman's eyes followed every movement and opened wide when she saw the twins. She finally pulled her glance away and stared at him again before speaking. "I came about the…" she said quietly, then collapsed in a heap on the floor.

Her eyes slowly opened, and she looked about. Jonah sat on the edge of the sofa next to her. His mother stood over her, making sure she was alright. "I still think we should get Doc Henderson out here," she said gruffly. "She is obviously not alright. Just look at her face."

The stranger began to sit up, then collapsed back onto the pillow Ma had put behind her head. "I'm sorry," the woman said quietly. "I should go."

Jonah reached out and took her hand. Instead of being soft as he expected, they were work roughened. She was not old, probably in her twenties. Far too young for her skin to be like this.

Looking beyond the bruises and the worry lines on her face, her beauty was evident.

"Please stay," he said, then reached out and gently touched the largest bruise – it covered her cheekbone and ventured up and over one eye. She flinched as his fingers connected ever so lightly. "When did this happen?" he asked, anger flaring within him. Whatever she did, if indeed she did anything, the young woman before him did not deserve this.

She licked her lips before answering, they looked parched. Ma handed her some water and she took a large mouthful. "Thank you," she said, glancing up at his elderly mother.

She handed the glass back and sat up. "My drunkard father," she said matter-of-factly. "He did it last night in a drunken stupor because he thought I didn't make his coffee." She fiddled with her hair and tried to tie it back up. "The empty mug was sitting on the counter."

She closed her eyes and swayed a little and Jonah thought she would collapse again. Instead she surprised him by standing.

He watched as she straightened her skirt and reached into the pocket. "I came about this," she said, this time sounding a little more confident. "You sent me a letter." She pulled his letter out of her pocket and waved it around. "Is the job still open?" She looked up at him with her big brown eyes in desperation.

"I, uh," Words failed him. "You're Faith Perkins?" It was the last thing he expected.

She folder his correspondence up again and put it back in her skirt pocket, then began to walk away. "Where are you going?" He was getting a headache, probably due to worry about her situation.

She glanced back over her shoulder as she headed toward the door. "I can see you are good people, and I don't want you caught up in this. My father and brother are sure to come looking." She licked her lips. "They are not the sort to take no for an answer."

That got his back up. "I can deal with the likes of them." And he would if it came to that. "Have you eaten? We were just about to have lunch."

"I, I…" He could see from her expression she was hungry but didn't want to impose.

Ma walked over to her and put a gentle arm around her shoulder. "You're safe her, Faith," she said quietly. "Besides, we need your help too."

"We do," Jonah said, and earned himself a scathing glance from his mother. He understood – Faith was like a scared rabbit and needed coaxing. Not that he blamed her after what she'd been through. He was willing to guess it wasn't the first time either.

Ma was right, she was safe here, and he would protect her no matter what.

"Sit down," Ma said, pulling a kitchen chair out for Faith. "The children have eaten already and are having their afternoon nap now."

Faith nodded, then glanced across at the food strewn over the table. She sat down as directed but didn't look comfortable.

Scared was more like it. She didn't know him or his mother and had no idea if she was safe here. Somehow he had to convince her she was.

"Do you prefer tea or coffee," Ma asked gently. She was keeping her voice low, and it seemed to be pacifying the young woman.

"Tea, please," she said quietly, then began to rise. "I, I really should go," she said, but suddenly his mother was by her side.

She leaned in close. "You're safe here, Faith. Don't be afraid. My name is Martha, I'm Jonah's mother." Faith nodded again, and Martha hugged her, but Faith flinched, pulling back.

The two women shared a look, which had Jonah confused until Faith pushed her sleeves up. His mother gasped at the appalling bruises that marred her overly thin arms.

Jonah swallowed. He had never witnessed anything so horrific in his life. His animals were treated better than this young woman had been. He vowed there and then it wouldn't happen again. He would take care of her.

These were good people, and Faith did not want to put them in danger.

They insisted she stay and eat, and it would be rude to deny their invitation, so she reluctantly stayed. She was fine until Martha came over and hugged her, that was her undoing, and it took all her resistance not to break into tears.

Not only had she had a long trip here, but the pressure of leaving the cottage as though it was just another day really got to her.

After nearly an hour of travel she'd begun to sob. At first she couldn't understand it, and no matter how hard she tried, she couldn't stop. She finally realized it was the relief of getting away unnoticed. Of course it was one thing to get away, but quite another to never be found.

"Faith?" She was lost in her thoughts and it was only Martha's kind voice that brought her back out again. "Would you like fried potatoes with your pancakes?"

At first she was confused and glanced about. The place was unfamiliar, until her gaze settled on the elderly woman who had been so kind to her. "Thank you, just a little," she said only slightly above a whisper.

She glanced across at Jonah who was sitting like the naughty child in the corner, and not saying a word. She owed him a huge apology for intruding into the tranquility of his family home.

"I am still looking for a housekeeper," he said, his voice lower than it was earlier. She glanced across at Martha who frowned at him.

"It's alright," she told the other woman. "I came about the position, after all."

He reached for his mug of coffee, then added fried potatoes and onions to his plate, as well as two fried sausages.

"I can cook and clean house," she said confidently. "I've been doing it for years. Of course, I can't give you references since I don't want anyone to know where I am."

The two stared at her. "No references required," Jonah finally said. "But there are things we need to discuss – if you're up to it, that is."

"That can surely wait until we finish eating," Martha chastised her son. "First we say a blessing, then we eat, *then* you can talk."

They joined hands and Martha began to pray. "Thank you for this food, Lord, and thank you for guiding Faith to us. Amen."

"Amen."

Faith looked up, barely able to control her emotions. She had never felt so loved in her life as she did with these total strangers.

After the meal was finished, Faith offered to help with the dishes, but Martha would have none of it. "You sit and talk with Jonah. You two have unfinished business," she said. "We need to get you settled in."

Settled in? That was a revelation. Jonah had not even discussed the possibility of working here yet. She had no idea what she was in for.

She sat on the sofa next to the fire, and he sat on the chair opposite. "Things became quite difficult after my wife Sarah died," he said quietly, then lowered his voice even more. "My mother is not up to looking after the house anymore, or the children," he said conspiratorially.

"How old are they?" She'd never dealt with children before, so if she got the position, things could get interesting.

"The twins are three," he said matter-of-factly. "Their names are Cora and Leo, and to be honest, after everything they've been through, their behavior is pretty good."

Pretty good? Did that mean what she thought it did? "I'd have to look after the children too? You didn't say that in the advertisement," she said, glancing across at Martha who had joined them.

"They are well-behaved children," Martha interjected. "I don't know why Jonah would say otherwise."

"Perhaps because they don't always do what I tell them to do."

Martha sighed. "They're three-years-old, Jonah. Three-year-olds don't always do what they're told."

He ignored his mother's words. "You can obviously clean house, and I think you said you can cook?" Faith wasn't sure why they were even having this conversation. It was obvious their minds had been made up the moment she walked through the door.

Their whole demeanor wreaked of desperation, as she was sure hers did too. She needed this job, and if she didn't get it, Faith had no idea what she would do. There was no way she could risk going back home. Next time her father could very well kill her.

"...start?"

What did she miss? "I'm sorry, what did you say?"

Jonah stared at her. "I said when can you start?"

Oh. She got the position. She should be rejoicing but there were other things to consider first. "That will depend on when I can find accommodation in town. I can't very well sleep in the buggy," she said, half joking.

Jonah and Martha stared at each other. "We have a spare room here," Jonah said quickly. "You can stay here. It will be far better than you paying rent and traveling twenty minutes both ends of the day."

She glanced from one to the other. "I, I couldn't," she said. "For one, it wouldn't be proper. Secondly, I don't want to be an imposition."

"I guess I could stay for a while," Martha said. That solved the propriety issue.

Jonah smiled and seemed relieved. "You have no idea how much it will mean to me if you take the position and stay here. Rent free of course."

She couldn't help but grin. "I am happy to work for free room and board," she said, feeling happier than she had for a very long time. And safe. So very safe.

He reached over and held both her hands. "If you work for me, you get paid," he said. It was almost at that moment they were hit by what seemed like a whirlwind. The twins ran out into the sitting room still wearing their nightgowns. Cora rubbed at her eyes and ran straight to her father. Leo stopped abruptly in front of her.

"Who are you?" He didn't mince words but came right out with it. She liked him already.

"I'm Faith. Who are you," she asked, already knowing the answer.

He glanced across at his father, who nodded. "I'm Leo." He then joined his sister at their father's side.

"What happened to your face," Cora asked quietly.

"Cora," Jonah warned.

Cora stared at her momentarily. She deserved an answer. "I had an accident," she said quietly. The little girl ran to her side and hugged her tight.

Faith fought back tears. She had experienced more love in the short time she'd been here than she had since her mother had died. Warmth flooded her.

Chapter Three

Faith was shown to her new room. It wasn't much, Martha had told her, but she'd never seen Faith's own room back home.

This room had a single bed made of wrought iron, with a beautiful quilt laying on top. "The quilt was made by my own mother many years ago," she said, lifting the end of it and breathing in the fragrance. "It was made with love."

She glanced up at Faith and smiled as if remembering something very special. Faith could only imagine the memories that came with that quilt. "You can put your clothes in that wardrobe," she said. "This room has been unused for some time, so do what you want with it."

She opened the drapes and Faith looked out across the field. The view was amazing. Mountains surrounded them and were covered with trees and other foliage. Two fields over she could see what appeared to be a herd of cattle. "Does that land belong to Jonah?"

"It does. He owns all the land for miles around." She then pointed to a small dressing table next to the bed. "That is empty, so do use it. The mirror is old, but not too bad."

It was far better than the one Faith had used for over a decade. If only Martha knew what she'd endured. That said, she already feared the older woman had realized.

"There's a chair in the corner you can use too. I'm afraid the lighting isn't the best. Do you knit?"

Faith's eyes opened wide at the question. "I don't – I've never had time to learn." She could elaborate but she was beginning to feel like a victim and that just wouldn't do.

"Jonah is getting your bags and the ranch hands will see to your horse and buggy. You don't need to worry yourself over them."

"I can't thank either of you enough," she said quietly as Jonah entered the room with her meagre belongings. "You've done more for me than anyone has ever done." She'd been through so much the past two days, and her emotions were running high, but Faith vowed not to show further vulnerability to these lovely people. She'd done far too much of that already.

Martha stepped forward to hug her, but suddenly stepped back. Faith appreciated it given the pain she'd endured last time.

"We are happy to help, my dear. I'd like to think we are helping each other." She flashed that grandmotherly smile that had already helped Faith feel at home with these people. "Why don't you lay down and have a rest. You look plumb tuckered out."

Jonah, who hadn't said a word to this point, interjected. "Ma's right. You look exhausted. Lay down and sleep."

The pity on his face riled her, but she knew he meant well. Her first assessment was correct she was sure. They were good people, and she was safe here.

Faith took off her boots and lay on the bed fully dressed, while Martha closed the drapes again, putting the room in near darkness.

She was asleep almost the moment her head hit the pillow.

"Ssssssh. We're not supposed to wake her."

Faith opened her eyes a fraction and saw two pairs of eyes staring down at her.

"You shoosh. You're not the boss of me," Leo told his sister, his hands on his hips.

Faith couldn't help but grin. If this was an example of what it was like to have three-year-olds around, she was in for a treat.

The door was open about a quarter, and she could see light streaming down the hallway. She felt incredibly refreshed, which was surprising after such a short nap.

"Where have they gone?" Jonah's voice traveled through the house, and Cora put her fingers to her mouth as she giggled.

Footsteps carried down the hallway, and Martha quietly entered the room. "You two," she whispered, taking a hand of each child. "Out you go."

"But grandma," they said in unison. "Faith is awake."

Martha glanced down at her. "I'm so sorry, my dear. These little devils snuck away and we had no idea where they'd gone."

She swung her legs over the side of the bed, and the children stepped in to hug her around the waist. Warmth flooded her at the unselfish act.

"Supper will be ready soon," Martha told her.

"Supper? How…" She surely hadn't been asleep that long? "Why didn't you wake me? I could have helped."

"No need – you obviously needed to sleep. There is something I need to warn you about."

Her breath hitched in her throat. Had Father found her already? "Is it Father?" she asked in a small voice.

"Oh good gracious no! I'm sorry if I scared you." She stepped forward and gently put her arm around Faith's shoulders. "The ranch hands eat with us, so they'll all be in soon." She glanced at Faith and frowned. "Did my son remember to tell you that? You'll be cooking for them too – twice a day. We provide a hot breakfast and supper for our workers. They sometimes have the noon meal with us, but not often – they're usually out in the paddocks at that time of day."

Her mind was ticking over. How many men would she be cooking for? Why did she come here? She couldn't do this. Could she?

"We have three ranch hands, so not many. I'll be here to help for a while yet."

Did that mean Martha would be leaving? Would she be here alone with Jonah? That wasn't proper, it could ruin her reputation, what little there was left of it. Her father had seen to that with his very improper behavior.

She suddenly felt deflated. She'd come here to help the rancher, and he'd ended up helping her. She owed it to him to stay and at least give it a try.

As though she could read her mind, Martha began to reassure her. "You can do it; I know you can. Freshen yourself up and I'll see you in the kitchen." She flashed her a smile that made Faith believe everything was alright with the world.

The four men sat at the table, and all talk stopped abruptly as she walked into the room. They all suddenly stood and glanced her way.

"Ma'am," they all said at once.

She felt herself stiffen at the sudden attention. "Please don't stand on my account," she said suddenly feeling nervous.

The three ranch hands sat, but Jonah remained standing. "Faith, allow me to introduce you to my workers." He pointed to each man as he introduced him. "This is Hank Daley, my foreman, Percy Langmore, and Rory Constance."

She stared at them momentarily. Hank was in his forties, maybe even early fifties by the look of him, but the other two were far younger – mid-thirties at most. "Pleased to meet you," she said, then joined Martha before she could become more of a spectacle. No doubt Jonah had warned them not to mention her bruises or to stare, because none did either.

"See, that wasn't so bad, was it?" Martha whispered. "They are good men, all of them, and will see you are not harmed in any way."

She was right, it wasn't too bad. No doubt Jonah had told them all about her and her problems. She wanted to curl into a ball and cry, but that wasn't an option available to her. Martha's hand suddenly covered hers. "It will get easier, I promise."

Faith nodded. It surely would; it had to get better than it was today.

"These biscuits need to go on the table," Martha instructed. "And the butter." There were more biscuits than Faith had ever seen before. "These boys are big eaters," Martha said, reading her mind. "They work hard all day, and we feed them well."

She took the food to the table, and it was no sooner there, than hands reached out to grab it. "Fellas, a little decorum," Jonah said, chastising his men.

They all stared at him momentarily, then grinned, shoving the food into their mouths.

She hurried back to Martha. "Are they always like that?"

"Hungry, do you mean? Yes, they are."

She had her work cut out for her. Faith could see she would spend most of her day cooking for hungry men and would have little time for much else.

When the main meal was served, they joined hands and said the blessing. The children sat with them tonight.

"The children don't normally eat with us," Jonah explained. "I thought it would be nice for you to get to know each other."

"Good idea," she said, before reaching for a biscuit. She felt as though she hadn't eaten for days. "What time do they normally eat and go to bed?"

"They eat at five, and go to bed at seven," Martha said. "That way they get to spend time with their father."

"Of course," she said before taking a dainty bite of her food. The four men stared at her. She swiped at her mouth with a napkin. "Do I have food on my face," she asked as they continued to stare.

Martha rolled her eyes. "I'm sure it's because you're not eating like a pig, like this lot."

They all began to object at once. Faith couldn't stop herself from grinning. "You're going to fit right in here, my dear," the older woman said, then went back to her food.

"Leo, don't throw your food," Jonah said firmly.

Cora glanced across at him and grinned. Surely she wouldn't… Oh yes she would. She picked up a slice of bread and threw it at her father. Jonah was losing patience, that much was clear.

The three workers tried to hold back a grin but couldn't.

"Right, that's it," he said sternly, and picked them up, ready to put the two to bed Faith was sure. "This is why little children don't get to eat with the adults." It was obvious he was at the end of his tether.

Tears rolled down their little faces, and Faith couldn't help but feel bad for them.

"Do you mind if I try?" Faith asked quietly, not wanting to interfere, but also not wanting to see the two punished for being children.

"Be my guest." He deposited them away from the table where Faith could talk to them.

She pulled them aside and spoke quietly. "Would you like to play some games tomorrow? Something special?"

She looked into the little faces, and they stared back expectantly but said nothing. "Perhaps we could make something? A cake or some muffins."

"Muffins!" they both yelled, and Faith knew she'd found their favorite activity.

She smiled. "Then no more throwing food or misbehaving. If you can do that for me, we'll make muffins tomorrow."

They stared at each other then nodded. Finally, they hugged.

Faith envied the relationship the twins had with each other. She wished she'd had a twin or a sibling who she could have a relationship with. Not Martin, that was for sure. He showed his true colors from the day their father took him to the hotel for the first time.

"Are we ready to go back to the table and behave? Remember what I said."

"Muffins!"

She couldn't help but laugh. Faith reached for their hands and they willingly took hers, then climbed up at the table when they returned. Whenever they looked like misbehaving, Faith reminded them of their promise. They grinned at her and behaved like perfect angels.

"What did you tell them?" Jonah asked as they sat in the sitting room later that night after the children had been put to bed. "I've never seen them so well behaved."

She laughed, and he liked the sound her laughter made. It was the first time he'd seen her laugh, and it made him feel good.

"It was easy – I worked out what they like to do and bribed them with it. Behave at the table or miss out."

Very clever. "It apparently worked. You're good with children – you must have heaps of experience with them."

Heat rose in her cheeks and he wondered why. His curiosity got the better of him, but he said nothing. Jonah moved toward the fire and stoked it, throwing some small logs on it.

"I, I've never had anything to do with children," she admitted, and he was shocked. Faith seemed competent, but that now proved to be a fluke. Could he trust her with his children while he was away for the day working?

He took a deep fortifying breath.

He had to trust her. He needed to feel confident in her ability to run the household without him. Besides, his mother promised to stay around for at least another week or two, and he would hold her to her word.

She suddenly went pale. "Is that a problem," she asked tentatively. "Because if it is, I'll move on."

His head shot up. "No! I need you here, and you need somewhere to stay."

The color slowly came back into her cheeks. "Thank you," she said quietly. "I don't know what I would do if not for you."

"The feeling is reciprocated." He sat staring at her for some minutes. "You didn't say when you wanted to start. Perhaps in a week, to give yourself time to recover?"

She closed her eyes tightly then opened them. "I'd planned on tomorrow, if that suits you."

He began to object, but she put her hand up to stop him. "I am fine, I promise. Besides, Martha promised to help me, so it's not as though I'll be suddenly thrown in the deep end."

How could he argue with that? The woman had principles. Whether or not she was a good housekeeper and cook as she said she was, remained to be seen.

Chapter Four

Faith rolled out of bed at five. Today was no different to any other day except she had more mouths to feed.

Martha had shown her where to find everything and outlined what she needed to do. She'd insisted the older woman stay in bed.

Talk about finding herself in the midst of chaos, but it was of her own doing. If she didn't do it now, she would have to take the plunge sometime.

The kettle was near boiling, and she had all the mugs lined up on the counter. The bacon was cooking along with nearly a dozen eggs. The toast was keeping warm in the oven, along with the sausages.

She had butter on the table, and the table was set. She expected the men any minute. Faith hoped they didn't make too much noise and wake the children, but Martha promised they wouldn't. They'd been doing this for long enough not to wake them, she'd said.

She glanced across at the fire and sighed. She hadn't done as good a job with the fire as she'd hoped, so crossed the floor to stoke it some more, it was growing dim. It was the one thing she hadn't been able to control this morning. Everything else had been running smoothly.

"Here, let me." Jonah's voice came out of nowhere, and it startled her. He stared into her alarmed face. "I'm sorry," he said quietly. "I didn't mean to startle you."

She stood as he crouched down, then stared as the muscles in his back rippled as he got the fire going as it should be. As much as she tried, she couldn't pull her eyes away. He was a wonderful specimen of a man – surely the best she'd ever encountered.

"Something smells good," he said as he stood, pulling her thoughts back to the food, then crossed the floor to the stove.

She stared out the window at the sunrise, ashamed of her feelings of just moments ago. "The sunrise is beautiful," she said as she continued to stare.

"Yes, it is," he said, about to pour himself a coffee.

"Here, let me." Their hands touched as she tried to pick up the mug he was holding, ready to make his morning beverage. Warmth flooded her.

He glanced at her, and she felt heat flood her face. "You're not my slave," he said quietly. "You're no one's slave. Remember that."

This was something totally new to Faith and she wasn't sure how to process it. She'd been treated like a slave by her various employers, and even more so by her father.

She studied him momentarily then nodded, and finally let him pour his own coffee. Moments later the workers came inside, kicking their boots off at the door, and hanging their hats on the pegs that were placed there for that very purpose.

"Good morning," she said brightly, trying to block out her feelings of just moments ago. "Take a seat and I'll get your coffee." She glanced across at Jonah who stared at her. Was it in disapproval after their conversation of just moments ago?

"Good morning," they said back, none the wiser.

They all sat down as directed, and Faith already knew she was going to love working here, but also knew she had to keep her distance from her new boss. She felt a connection with him that she was convinced she shouldn't feel.

It had been a busy morning.

After cleaning up from the men's breakfast, Faith began work on a beef stew for supper. There was an abundance of produce available, and Martha had insisted she use whatever she needed. It was a nice change after using the least amount of everything back home.

Even some of her cleaning clients were penny-pinchers, not to mention her father.

With the stew now on the stove cooking, she began to prepare for the morning break. Jonah said they'd be working close to the ranch house today, so would be in for coffee around nine. She decided to surprise them.

Faith hadn't had a break all morning, and now she could hear the children moving about. This was far more challenging than she'd envisioned, but she would push on.

She refilled the kettle for a much-needed cup of tea, then quietly went to their bedroom, not wanting to disturb Martha. Their grandmother was not young and had been running this extremely busy household for quite some time.

She deserved a sleep in.

She opened the children's door a crack to see what they were up too. Still in their nightgowns, they were jumping up and down on their beds. She could only imagine what Jonah would say.

"Faith!" they both squealed when they spotted her. "I'm hungry."

She couldn't help but grin. They were so sweet, even if they were a bit naughty at times.

As she opened the door, they came running toward her and hugged her legs. She felt moved by the unconditional love these toddlers showed her, and worried if she didn't end up staying. Jonah had promised nothing, and she was yet to prove to him she was up to the job.

She hadn't yet convinced herself she was either.

After helping the two choose their clothes for the day, and helping them dress, she combed Leo's hair, then brushed Cora's hair and began to braid it.

"Papa always hurts me when he brushes my hair." She pouted as she spoke.

"Poor little Cora. Well I'm here now, and I won't hurt you."

Cora spun around in her arms and hugged Faith tightly. "I love you, Faith," she said quietly, then spun back for her hair to be finished.

Faith sat on the edge of the bed in surprise. Did the child really love her, or was it just something small children said? She really had no idea.

"I love you too," Leo said, not to be outdone, and finished it with a hug as well. Faith was beginning to see these two were in constant competition. It was both amusing and disconcerting.

She finished up with Cora's hair, then the three headed for the kitchen.

"Sit down and I'll get your breakfast," she insisted, then poured them each a cup of milk.

The twins exchanged a glance. "We have cookies for breakfast," Leo announced.

Faith glanced from one to the other. "I think you're trying to trick me," Faith said, and the twins erupted into laughter. "I've made oats for you," Faith said gently. "Your grandma told me that's what you have."

"It is indeed what they have." Until now, Martha's presence had gone unnoticed. "Good morning, Faith," she said. "I hope you slept well."

She glanced up and smiled at the woman who had become something of a mentor. "Thank you, I did. Coffee?"

She didn't wait for an answer, instead pulling a mug from the cupboard and placing the filled mug in front of Martha at the table.

She dished out a small bowl of oats for each of the children and placed it in front of them.

"I can't feed myself," Leo said with a serious face.

"Me neither," said Cora.

Faith frowned.

"Take no notice," Martha said. "They have their Papa fooled, but they feed themselves all the time when he's not around."

The twins began to laugh until they almost cried – their little hands covering their mouths as they bent forward. It seemed they liked to play tricks on her.

"Well, I expect no more of that," Faith said sternly, then turned to the sink before the children saw her grin.

By the time she turned back, the twins had finished eating and were huddled together. It worried her. She glanced across at Martha who was watching them carefully. "They tend to plot things to do," she said with a touch of mirth in her voice. "They don't usually do much harm though."

Checking the time, Faith put a tray into the oven. Another half hour or so before the workers would return for coffee. She filled the kettle – it felt as though that's all she did lately – then set the mugs out for their drinks.

"Papa will be soon home for coffee," Martha told the twins, and they jumped up and down excitedly. "Go and tidy yourselves up."

They immediately ran toward their room.

"How do you like it so far," Martha asked once the twins were gone.

Faith sighed. "I haven't stopped all morning, and to be honest, I'm worn out already." She slumped down into a chair opposite the older woman with a mug of tea.

Martha reached out and covered her hand, patting it as she spoke. "I'm sure you'll get used to it. Give yourself some time to get into a routine."

Faith glanced up at her and nodded. "I'll try."

"Please," Martha implored her. "We really need you. Desperately need you. At least give us a week or two before you make a decision." She held Faith's hand tightly. "I'm not sure what we'll do if you leave."

Frowning, Faith studied her. "Is it really that bad?" Perhaps she didn't truly understand the situation. "Besides, I have nowhere else to go." It really was that simple. She would have to make this work because above all, she couldn't go home. Not ever.

Suddenly it hit her.

It was far too quiet, and the twins were out of sight. What were they up to?

Making her way to their bedroom, Martha followed. "They're little tricksters," Martha said. "They always have some little scheme to fall back on."

Faith opened the bedroom door but saw nothing. She looked under the bed; they weren't there. Could they have climbed in the wardrobe? She certainly hoped not – they could possibly suffocate in there.

Her heart was pounding, and she felt suddenly ill. Where on earth could they be?

"Cora, Leo, where are you?"

She heard the faintest of giggles but couldn't work out where it was coming from. Until she noticed the movement of the bed coverings.

She quietly went over to the bed and began to tickle. Two heads popped out, still giggling.

Such fun! Faith couldn't remember a time she'd had such fun since she was a small child herself. She glanced across at their grandmother who clearly didn't approve. "I hope they stop this nonsense soon," she said. "This behavior can be quite wearing."

Those few words confirmed Faith's fears – the children were far too much for Martha. She just hoped she could sustain working here and take over from the older woman.

"Right, out of bed you two. Time to make your beds." She first made Leo's bed, since the children were still in Cora's, then made the second bed.

Faith picked up a few toys scattered around the room and returned them to their rightful place – the toybox. "From now on, toys must be returned to the toybox when you finish playing." She kept her voice stern, but gentle.

"Yes Faith," they both said, their eyes downcast.

She threw open the drapes to let the light in, then closed the door behind them.

The kitchen smelled divine, and she wondered if the workers would appreciate her little surprise. She hadn't made oat cookies for far too long. She'd always enjoyed baking but didn't usually have the time. Or the inclination.

Hopefully that would change.

She opened the oven a fraction, and saw her cookies were ready. She snatched up a couple of kitchen towels and pulled the hot tray from the oven and placed it on a wooden board on the counter. She reached for a cake cooler from the cupboard and taking them off the oven tray, sat them there to cool.

It wouldn't be long and the menfolk would arrive. She wanted her cookies ready to eat by the time they sat down.

She lined the mugs up ready for their coffee and took a large platter from the cupboard. It wasn't long before she heard screams of excitement. "Papa, Papa!"

She continued with her preparations, the enticing smell making her hungry. She felt his presence before she knew Jonah was standing directly behind her at the counter.

His hands sat either side of her on the countertop and his body brushed up against hers as he leaned in. "They smell delicious," he said into her ear. "You didn't have to go to all this trouble."

"Yes, she did," Hank yelled. "I won't say no." She heard his laughter and knew he was joking.

"Thank you," Jonah said quietly, and she cranked her head back to look at him. She hadn't realized how tall he was before. Possibly since he'd sat most of the time they'd talked.

She spun around to look at him properly. "You're welcome," she said. "I'm not sure you'll get this every day, but I don't mind baking. In fact, I enjoy it most of the time."

She stared into his eyes. They were the bluest eyes she'd ever seen, and she was totally mesmerized. She finally pulled her gaze away. "I'd better get these on the table and pour the coffee," she said quietly, then slipped out from under his arms.

Heat was zinging around her body. What was it about this man that caused such a reaction in her?

It had to be his kindness. No one had ever been so kind to her before.

Faith decided that had to be the answer. The longer she worked here, she was certain things would calm down. At least she hoped that would be the case. She already felt like she had feelings for her boss. Hopefully they were feelings of gratitude and nothing more.

Chapter Five

The twins were tucked up in bed sound asleep, and Faith was ready to drop.

She had no idea it would be so exhausting looking after two young children. It had been extra busy today, Martha told her, because the men were working close to the house. Normally they worked farther away, and wouldn't be in from breakfast until supper.

As selfish as it sounded to her, it also sounded like far less work. To be fair though, she'd caused a lot of the work herself. They hadn't expected anything more than coffee when they came in, but she'd insisted on making cookies.

Not a lot of work for sure, but it was added stress.

"Make yourself a cup of tea and take a break."

She glanced up to see Martha sitting on the sofa. "I might do that. Thanks."

"Better yet, why don't you lay down and rest while the terrible two sleep?"

Could she? Did she even dare? What if Jonah came in and found her sleeping on the job? It was tempting, but she couldn't afford to lose her job after only one day. "I can't," she said quietly. "I might lose my job."

"My dear girl," Martha said, wriggling about, trying to get comfortable. "Jonah has done what you're doing now. He will completely understand. Besides," she said, finally happy with her seating. "You look ready to drop. You won't last until supper the way you're going."

She was totally right and Faith knew it. She checked the stew that was slowly cooking on the stove, and stirred it.

She refilled the kettle and added it to the stove, but not before stoking the wood fire stove and ensuring it had enough fuel.

Martha studied her. "My dear girl, if you don't go soon, it won't be worth bothering."

"You're right, of course you are. I just feel so guilty…"

"Stop it! There is nothing to feel guilty about. Now go." Martha grinned at her. If she hadn't done so, Faith would have felt like a child being chastised by an overbearing parent.

"I'm going," she said, then headed to her bedroom with a smile. Closing the drapes to hopefully help her sleep in the middle of the day, Faith pulled off her apron, and then her boots. Lastly she removed her gown and lay it across the chair in the corner.

She threw back the bedding and climbed in. It felt like she was floating on air, the mattress was so comfortable. But she realized it was also because she was beyond exhausted.

She closed her eyes and was soon fast asleep.

"Is she dead?" The harshly whispered words shattered the tranquility of Faith's dreams. She opened one eye.

"I hope not." Leo's distraught voice made her heart thud.

She opened the other eye. "I'm not dead," she said, still half asleep.

"I'll get Jonah to put a lock on this door. You don't want these two waking you when they're up and about." Martha stood in the doorway watching the children stand over her.

"It's perfectly fine," she said, pulling the bedding up around her shoulders. "I can't believe I slept so long. It must be getting late."

Another hour or so and it will be supper time," Martha said. "You obviously needed the sleep, like I thought." She smiled briefly. "I stirred the stew for you, and didn't let it burn."

Faith's heart rate accelerated. "I'm supposed to be making your life easier, not the other way around."

She was totally distraught. How could she have slept for so long? "Oh my gosh, I have biscuits to make," she said, suddenly in a panic. "I knew I shouldn't have laid down. Now I'm behind in my chores." She was getting a headache just thinking about it.

"Faith, it's not a problem," Martha said, shooing the children out of the room so Faith could dress in peace. She was grateful for the privacy.

After dressing she pulled the drapes aside. The sky was already darkening – she would have to work quickly if she was to get the biscuits made and in the oven in time for supper.

She still couldn't believe she could sleep so long. It mustn't happen again. She would not let herself be talked into resting in the middle of the day again.

Making her way to the kitchen, the chill in the air hit her. She glanced across to see the fire had died down. She squatted down to get it going again and was reminded of the last time she'd done this very same thing.

Heat rose in her cheeks as she remembered the feelings she'd had watching Jonah. She threw some twigs on the fire, and lit a screwed up newspaper, trying to get the fire started. Faith found it frustrating as she'd done it many times before, but here it wasn't working.

She took a deep breath.

This time she tried to calm herself down. Everything here was new to her and she was nervous. Perhaps she was trying too hard? Whatever was causing it, Faith found it frustrating. She picked up the fire iron and stoked the fire. She could see the burning embers and shoved some twigs into them.

Slowly she added the newspaper that had earlier refused to cooperate. Finally the fire began to burn. She was mesmerized by the flames. This time two days ago she was worrying about being injured from her father's brutal attacks. Today she was feeling safe, and even loved, in a home where she was needed and wanted.

She threw a small log on the fire and waited for it to catch alight. Faith now knew she had been inpatient. Something she'd long been known for. In the past though, she was impatient for what amounted to freedom.

Adding a couple more smaller logs, she had to trust the fire to keep alight without her assistance. She needed to get those biscuits made and in the oven. She hoped the fire in the stove was burning nicely, otherwise she'd really be in strife.

She almost ran there, and discovered it burning beautifully – exactly how she needed it to be.

Faith gathered up all her ingredients and a large bowl. She was cooking for far more than usual, not to mention these were hungry men, and they ate a lot.

Closing the oven door she heard the back door open, and she went into a panic. She stirred the stew, which was going well, and quickly set the table. She filled the kettle and prepared the crockery ready for the food to be dished out.

She already had the children's food cooling. Would Jonah challenge her over the decision to let the children eat with the adults?

Her heart fluttered when she glanced up to see him studying her. "Faith," he said with a nod of his head.

"Hello, Jonah," she said, then busied herself with the meal preparations.

She felt his presence near her before she knew for certain he was next to her. "The children said they thought you were dead today." There was the slightest hint of a smile to his face.

She wasn't sure what was so funny about it.

"I'll put a lock on your door tomorrow. You don't want little intruders while you sleep."

She prepared herself for a backlash. "I, I shouldn't have been sleeping. It won't happen again."

He frowned. "Why not? Those two are exhausting. Might as well rest while they do. My wife always did that."

He stepped closer and stared into her eyes. So close she could feel the heat from his body. "You need your privacy," he said quietly. "I appreciate you being here, Faith." His gaze went down to her lips and she licked them. "Today was the first time in a long time I wasn't worried about the children while I worked."

She glanced up into his eyes. "Really?" He trusted her that much already?

"Yes, really. Ma is beyond it. I always worry when she's alone with the little ones. What if something happened to her like…" He suddenly stopped and his face went pale, then he looked away.

It was clear to Faith that something terrible had happened, but she wasn't going to push him. "You can trust me to care for your children," she said gently, and put a hand to his arm. Heat surged through her, and he turned his head to stare at her hand.

He covered it with his own. "Faith," he said in her ear.

"Papa, Papa!" The twins came running across to him, wanting to be picked up. "You're home, Papa! I missed you," Cora said.

"I missed you too," Leo shouted, not wanting to be outdone.

The moment was lost, but Jonah studied her until the moment he turned away toward his children. Had he also felt the connection?

She shook her head. They were almost strangers, and had known each other for less than two days. There was no way there was any sort of connection is such a short period of time. Faith convinced herself her imagination was way out of control, brought about by nervous shock.

The back door being thrown open brought her back into the moment. The biscuits must be near to ready. She checked the oven; they were almost done.

She put a slab of butter on the table, filled the coffee mugs, and began to dish out the beef stew.

"That smells mighty good," Percy said to no one in particular. "No offence to you, Martha," he quickly added.

"None taken," Martha said with a frown. "I never once made beef stew." She stared at him as though daring him to say otherwise.

It was all Faith could do not to laugh. "I, I thought the children could eat with us tonight," she told Jonah. "Their food is already cooled."

He stared at her as he continued to hold the terrible two, then stared at each of them consecutively. "Will you behave?" he asked them, or should you go to bed now?"

Cora put her little fingers to her Papa's cheek. "I'm hungry, Papa," she told him.

"Me too," Leo added.

"Your face is sharp, Papa," Cora added, which made Jonah grin.

"As long as you promise to behave, you can eat with the adults." He glanced across at Faith. "It can be an experiment for now. If it doesn't work out, we'll go back to feeding them separate from the adults."

She agreed. *Besides, what choice did she have?*

With everyone seated at the table, Faith began to serve out the food, placing a plate of stew in front of each adult. She then served the children their supper. "This should be perfect. Not too hot," she told them.

Leo stared down into his food, then swooped down with his hand and picked up a mouthful, shoving it into his mouth.

"Leo!" Faith's voice stopped all chatter at the table. "We do not eat with our hands." She took a dish cloth to him and cleaned his hand. "Use your spoon.

You cannot sit at the table with the adults if you don't eat nicely."

Leo bent his head. "Yes, Faith. Sorry, Faith," he said, sounding remorseful.

Jonah was watching the exchange very carefully. Was he unhappy she had scolded Leo? He didn't look unhappy, although he did seem annoyed at first.

But now he nodded slightly and grinned at her. Perhaps he didn't mind after all.

"Oh, my biscuits!" she shouted, and rounded to the oven. "I hope they're not burned."

She opened the oven door to find them slightly browner than she would normally be happy with, but they weren't burned, and that was the main thing.

She grabbed the platter and placed them all on it.

"Faith, for goodness sakes," Jonah said, sounding exasperated. "Sit down and eat."

She placed the platter on the table. "But I have to make the coffee," she said, leaning so close to him she could feel his breath.

"Everyone can make their own coffee, right fellas?" He looked around the table.

"Right."

"Of course."

"Mmmm," Hank said as he chewed. "For sure," he said when his mouth was empty.

She stared at Jonah, and saw his determination. "Sit." She didn't argue.

Chapter Six

With the children tucked up in bed, the adults sat in front of the fire.

Everyone helped themselves to coffee since Jonah would not allow Faith to become a slave to them all.

There were enough cookies left over from this morning for them to each have at least one. The fire was burning beautifully, and between the heat and the crackling sound, Jonah was beginning to doze.

Faith was constantly up and down from her chair, not able to relax. He opened one eye. "What is wrong with you," he asked groggily. "You never sit still. Me, I am glad for the downtime."

"Me too," Hank said.

She glanced across at him, appearing slightly annoyed. "There's nothing wrong with me," she said sounding testy. "I'm just making sure everything is done that needs to be done." She reluctantly sat back down again.

Jonah had no sooner closed his eyes than she was up and about again. He reached out and grabbed her hand as she walked past. "Faith," he whispered, pulling her closer. "What is going on?"

He didn't mean to sound annoyed, but he was concerned for her. She had worked non-stop all day, and now that it was evening, she was still trying to work.

She looked down at him, then at their entwined hands. "I'm not used to having spare time," she whispered, obviously hoping no one else would hear.

"I'm off to bed," Martha suddenly announced. "Goodnight everyone," she said as she left the room.

"We're off too," Hank said, staring out the other two workers.

Jonah was glad for their hindsight in understanding he wanted some privacy with Faith.

When the room was finally cleared, he sat up, now wide awake, and indicated for her to sit down opposite him. "I have no idea what you've been through," he said quietly, still holding her work-worn hands. "But I can tell life has not been kind to you."

She averted her eyes as he spoke and he knew the conversation was an uncomfortable one for her. "The last thing I want is for you to work yourself to an early grave."

Faith squirmed in her seat and still refused to look at him, causing him even more frustration. "Faith," he said quietly, then gently held her chin and turned her to face him.

"Are you sending me away," she whispered, tears brimming in her eyes.

"What? No." He frowned. Why would she even think that? "It's the last thing I want." He reached out and wiped away a tear as it trickled down her face. "Already your presence here has made my life easier. Not to mention the twins adore you."

He stared into those sad brown eyes, and it made his heart ache. What she'd endured he could only imagine, but it was obvious none of it was good.

The loathsome black bruise on her face was slowly turning purple and would take some time to fade away completely. It was a pity the recollections of her former life would never disappear from her memory.

A slight smile formed on her face. "Really?"

He sighed. "Really. What I want from you, is for you to slow down. Do less." She glanced away again.

"I, I'm not sure I can." Her voice began to crack, and he realized he'd pushed her too hard. If her life had been as difficult as he believed, she'd likely been programmed to work non-stop. It would be difficult to change that mentality.

Sitting on the edge of the sofa, holding hands like this, he felt a comfort he'd not felt for a very long time. He wanted nothing less than for her to sit next to him and snuggle in.

He longed to hold her close, but knew he shouldn't. Faith had come here to work for him, not to have a relationship with him.

She suddenly stood. "I need to tidy up before I go to bed," she said quietly, and headed toward the kitchen.

He stared up at her. It was going to be a long hard process to bring her back to anything like normality. He wasn't convinced it was even possible.

"Faith," he called gently. "Let me help you."

She stared at him for long moments in the firelight, and he was convinced she would refuse his offer. Finally she nodded and continued on her way. He followed two steps behind until they reached the kitchen.

He glanced about. There was almost nothing to be done. There was only the handful of mugs they'd used for their coffee and the platter which held the remainder of the oat cookies. His heart shattered. She'd been conditioned to be nothing less than a slave.

She poured water from the kettle into the sink, and washed the few mugs there. He dried and put them away.

As she turned away from the sink he noticed the tears pouring down her face. "Faith? What's wrong?"

She shook her head as if to dismiss him. "No one has ever helped me before," she said in a whisper. He pulled her to him and she cried against his chest. He wrapped his arms around her protectively, and hers slid up his back.

Warmth flooded his entire body and he knew in that moment he was right where he wanted to be. He also knew just because he wanted it, did not mean it was right.

He kissed the top of her head, wishing it was her lips he was kissing. Her arms slowly slid from around him and she pushed herself away. "I'm sorry," she said, then ran from his arms to her bedroom.

He heard the door close quietly behind her. Adrenaline rushed through his body and he knew he had no hope of sleeping now.

He poured himself another coffee and shrugged on his heavy coat, then went outside into the cold night air. Perhaps that would force some sense into him.

Hank stood outside the bunkhouse smoking. He crunched his cigarette with his boot and wandered over. "Is it that bad, boss?" His voice held some mirth, which only managed to annoy Jonah.

"No," he answered. "It is far worse."

Faith woke at the crack of dawn as she always did.

The memory of being held by Jonah sent warmth shimmering through her. She'd never been held like that before, never been comforted by anyone except her mother, and now she was gone.

But it was different with Jonah. It wasn't like the sort of hugs her mother had given her. This hug seemed to have a special meaning. Not like a regular hug, *a feel better* hug. This one seemed to send some sort of message.

If she didn't know better, Faith would think it was Jonah's way of telling her he had feelings for her. And not just the type a boss had for his housekeeper.

She lay in bed as she contemplated all of this information. It was all very new to her, and she wasn't even convinced it was true.

Until now she'd denied her feelings toward Jonah. He was her boss after all, and that was the way it had to stay. She was here to clean house, cook, and look after his adorable children, nothing more.

She pulled the bedding higher and snuggled in for just a moment, then felt guilty for not getting out of bed immediately. It was what she should have done the moment she awoke.

She glanced around the room – she might have only been here a matter of days, but it already felt like home. Faith slid out of bed and dressed, then threw back the drapes.

This time of day was special and she adored it. Serenity surrounded her, and she took comfort in it.

She brushed her hair then pinned it up, ready for the new day. As she stared through her bedroom window, the sun began to rise from behind the mountains. Nature was incredible, and she would never get enough of it.

But alas, she must. She had a full day ahead of her, and needed to get started. As quietly as she could manage, Faith tiptoed down the hallway toward the kitchen, then stoked the wood fire stove, getting the fire burning ready for breakfast. She filled the kettle and turned toward the main fire.

That was when she noticed him.

Jonah sat close to the fire, in the very chair he'd sat in last night. He was asleep, a half-filled mug of coffee balancing in his his lap. The fire was barely alight.

Dare she go over there and get the fire burning properly?

It was chilly, as it always was at this time of the morning. It was after all, winter. She quietly made her way toward the fire and used the fire iron to stir up some of the embers, keeping the noise level low. She glanced back over her shoulder to check she hadn't disturbed Jonah and found him staring down at her.

"I, I'm sorry," she said guiltily. "I didn't mean to wake you."

He pulled himself up to a proper sitting position. "I was half awake already," he said, placing the mug on a side table. "I couldn't sleep last night."

She stared at him. "Did you even go to bed?" Now she felt even more guilty. Was she the cause of his unrest? That sounded vain and she admonished herself.

Jonah sat there staring at her. Watching her every move. "No. No, I didn't."

She frowned and he continued to stare. "Why not?" She shifted under his intense scrutiny, then glanced away. "Sorry, that's not my business," she said quietly.

The fire was beginning to take hold, and she threw a small log onto the flames. "Here, let me," he said, as he came beside her and squatted to her level.

His body warmth surrounded her and she wanted nothing more than to be held by him. But that was the last thing she should be thinking. Her mind was fighting with the demands of her body. Jonah had comforted her in her time of need – there was nothing more to it.

At least that's what she told herself.

He worked the fire until he got it burning properly, then turned to face her. "About last night…"

She turned away from him and stood. The last thing she needed was to analyze what happened. She swallowed hard and glanced down at him. "It was nothing," she said flippantly. "I was upset, you comforted me."

He stared at her momentarily. Did he see through her façade? "There was far more to it than that." She watched as he licked his lips then swallowed hard. "At least there was for me."

As there was for her, but Faith had no intention of admitting it. She'd come here to escape her abusive father. Nothing more.

If she and Jonah became romantically involved, what then? Would he simply discard her when he'd had enough of her? She knew for certain if they did become involved and it didn't work out, she'd have to leave.

She wouldn't want to stay anyway if he broke her heart. Right now she was vulnerable, she knew it was true. Perhaps this was all born out of her vulnerability than anything else.

He shifted his stance and she was suddenly aware of the intensity of his gaze as he waited for her answer. When she didn't, he spoke. "I don't believe you." His words were a challenge and they both knew it.

"Then I don't know what to tell you," she said quietly, and turned to walk away. He gently caught her arm and pulled her back to him. She glanced up into his unshaven face and his disheveled hair. His eyes bore into her until she wrenched her eyes away.

"I, I can't do this," she said softly.

He looked suddenly saddened. "Is it me?" he asked gently. "I thought there was something between us?" He continued to stare at her and she melted under his gaze.

"It's not you. I, I…" How did she even say it? "I've never been held by a man before. It scares me."

His gaze deepened, then he grinned. Suddenly his arms reached out and pulled her closer. "Don't be scared," he said gently. "It can be a beautiful thing."

She glanced up at him, at his uncharacteristic state of unkemptness and stared. He was a handsome man, there was no doubt about it. "Faith," he whispered, as if warning her something was about to happen, then leaned down and kissed her.

Her heart pounded and her head exploded. No one had told her how special a man's kiss could be.

The kiss was gentle, and his lips were warm. He tasted of coffee and smelled of smoke from the fire. His arms tightened, and despite being terrified about the whole situation, she felt truly at home with Jonah.

He wouldn't harm her, she was certain of that, and finally relaxed into him. He pulled away and gazed at her. "Everything alright?" he whispered.

She managed a tiny smile. "Everything is perfect," she said, and he kissed her again.

Chapter Seven

The kettle boiled and Faith set out the coffee mugs. As the men poured into the house, she began to dish out their breakfasts – scrambled eggs with bacon, sausages, and toast.

Jonah had sat her down and gone through a few things with her before anyone else was up and about. He talked about her slowing down. Everything did not have to be done at once, or on the same day.

She could sit and rest whenever she wanted; he didn't expect her to work non-stop all day. And she absolutely did not have to make coffee for anyone. If she kept the water hot in the kettle, he'd be happy.

It was a far cry from what she'd been forced to do since she was barely a teenager.

She put a filled plate in front of each man, Jonah included. He glanced up and smiled at her. Faith felt the heat rise up her cheeks, and backed away from the table. He reached out and held her hand, then kissed the back of it.

She'd never been more embarrassed in her life.

Or perhaps she had. Either way the snickers from the three workers had her retreating. "Fellas," Jonah warned, his voice stern, and the taunting ended immediately.

When Faith sat at the table with her own meal, they said a blessing. Jonah's touch sent a shiver through her, making it hard to concentrate on the words he was saying.

"This is good," Hank said, his mouth half-full.

Percy agreed. "Don't tell Martha, but you are a far better cook than she is." He glanced up at Jonah, suddenly worried.

"I agree," Jonah said, a grin on his face. "But I wouldn't dare tell my mother." He glanced back over his shoulder to ensure she wasn't there. He sighed with relief when she wasn't.

"Should I expect you mid-morning today, or are you working farther away?" Faith glanced around the table, but everyone had their mouths full.

"We're working in the front paddock this morning. We'll be in for coffee, probably around nine." Jonah gulped down the last of his coffee and stood. "Breakfast was wonderful," he said. "Thank you."

"Oats most mornings becomes a bit monotonous," Rory added, then swallowed down the last of his coffee too."

"Plates in the sink, fellas. Faith is not your slave." Jonah glanced across at her and winked, reassuring her it was not a problem. He walked over to her, and kissed her on the cheek, then pulled her in and wrapped his arms around her.

"Jonah," she whispered fiercely. "People are watching."

Instead of answering, he covered her mouth with his and a shudder went through her. "I know," he whispered back when he'd finished kissing her. "See you in a few hours."

She really wanted to wipe that smirk off his face, and the best way to do that was to kiss him. But the men were already staring and grinning, so she decided to refrain. Besides, she still hadn't convinced herself she should be having a relationship with her boss.

With everyone gone, the house felt suddenly empty.

If she was truthful, it seemed that way because Jonah had gone. In the short time she'd been here, Faith had become accustomed to his presence.

She turned to the sink and began to prepare to wash the dishes. She poured in the boiling water from the kettle, which she quickly refilled, added the soap then some cold water so she didn't scald herself. Back home she had to go outside to pump the water, then cart heavy buckets of water into the house. Not once did Father or Martin help. They were too busy on the path to drunkenness.

Jonah's home had plumbing installed. She didn't even have to go outside for the privy. Everything was here in the house. She couldn't believe her luck.

She finished cleaning up the kitchen, then prepared a batter to make a pound cake to serve with the morning coffee.

It was in the oven cooking nicely and the children were still not awake, so Faith took Jonah's advise and made herself a mug of tea. She stoked the wood fire stove and threw in some more fuel, then sat down next to the fire in the sitting room.

She took a sip of tea, then leaned back and sighed.

How long had it been since she'd had a break like this? Thinking back, she realized it had never happened before. From the age of twelve, around the time her mother had died, Faith had been nothing but a slave to her ungrateful family.

Not only that, her father had sought outside work for her the moment she left school, and she'd been cleaning other people's homes ever since. It was nice to finally have a break. She knew it wouldn't be for long, since it was almost the time the twins awoke each morning. Once they did, they'd have her on her toes until their early afternoon nap time.

According to Jonah, that was a perfect time for her to take a break or have a nap as well.

All these changes to her routine had her head spinning. Even now, Faith felt there must be something she should be doing, but she promised Jonah she would resist the urge to work non-stop.

She took the last mouthful of her tea, and headed back to the kitchen to check on the cake. Opening the door just a fraction, she could see the cake was not quite ready, and closed the door again.

Without warning, the twins came running from their room toward her. "Faith!" They smashed into her legs, almost sending her toppling. She regained her balance, and leaned down to wrap her arms around them.

They had brought so much joy into her life, and Faith was more than pleased she had taken the risk to come all the way here to the Mountain Ridge Ranch. It was certainly a wonderful place to bring up children.

"Good morning," she said, then straightened up. "Your breakfast will be ready in a few minutes. Sit down and have some milk." She poured the milk, this time giving them only half a cup each. Faith had learned the hard way, a full cup was far too much for them to handle.

She stirred their oats, then dished it out into a bowl. "It's a little hot yet, so be very careful."

Cora and Leo nodded their little heads. "Can we make muffins today," Cora asked, her little face full of hope. "We didn't do it yesterday."

"I know, and I'm sorry. After breakfast, and when you are dressed, we'll make muffins."

"Yay!" they both shouted, then tucked into their breakfast.

Once the kitchen was clean, she helped the twins choose their clothes and get dressed. They disappeared out of sight while she made their beds. *Surely they would be fine for a few minutes alone.*

Her pace quickened as she got closer to the kitchen and it was far too quiet. She stopped dead in her tracks at the sight before her.

The twins sat in the middle of the kitchen floor, each with a bowl balanced on their lap, and flour from one end of the kitchen to the other. Each bowl was filled with flour and goodness knew what else, as they sat there mixing their *muffins*.

"Oh my," she said out loud, trying to keep calm. Then she remembered the pound cake. She prayed it wasn't burned.

She grabbed the kitchen towels and opened the oven door. It was a little brown, but not burned. She lifted it out onto the wooden board that was there for exactly that reason.

Faith reached for the cake cooler and tipped the pound cake out onto the rack, then glanced back at the children.

They were completely covered in flour. She wondered what else they'd taken from the pantry, and her gut wrenched. What would Jonah say? She was supposed to be taking care of his children, not letting them get into such a mess.

She bent over to begin cleaning up the mess, and Leo clapped his hands with joy. Flour hit Faith in the face and she suddenly began coughing, then straightened, trying to get her breath back.

"Oh my." It was the only words she got out before the laughter began.

She glanced across to see Jonah and the workers standing close by, not even trying to quell their laughter.

"It's really not funny," she said sourly, lifting her apron to remove the flour from her face.

Jonah stepped closer. "You look really cute," he said quietly, then looked down at his children.

"Leo, Cora," he said sternly. "What do you think you are doing?"

They'd apparently not seen their father until now, because the two began to squeal. "Papa!" they both screeched, and jumped up, toppling the bowls and their contents. They stared at their father for a heartbeat then began to run toward their bedroom.

"Oh no you don't," he said, reaching out and grabbing each child by the collar. He was trying to hold back his laughter, but Faith could see he was having a hard time controlling himself.

The children both looked down at their feet, and Jonah dropped down to their level. "Look at me." The twins complied. "That was not a nice thing to do."

"But Papa," Cora said.

"We're making muffins," Leo finished.

Jonah glanced up at Faith. "Is that right?" he said, then gazed at the children again. "I think you need to apologize to Faith. Look at this mess you have made."

"I'm sorry," Faith told him. "I said we would make muffins. I only took my eyes off them for a few minutes while I made their beds."

He held up his hand. "This is not your fault." He turned to the children. "I'm waiting."

The pair turned to face Faith. "Sorry, Faith," they said together, sounding very remorseful, but the hint of a smile played on their little faces.

Faith leaned down to pick up the bowls at the same time Jonah did, and their hands met. "I'm sorry," he whispered. "I did warn you they could be naughty. But this is far from acceptable."

He turned to the children again. "You two sit on the floor over there until we can get you cleaned up." Without another word, the children did as they were told.

With the mess cleaned up, Faith began to cut the now cooled pound cake so the workers could eat then get back to work. "I'm really sorry," Faith said again, and turned to place the cake on the table.

Jonah smiled at her, then reached out and gently brushed her cheek. "You still have flour on your face," he said. She lifted her apron to wipe it away, but made it worse. He reached around her to grab a kitchen towel, and his body brushed against hers.

He stared into her eyes as he removed the last of the flour. "That's better," he said, then leaned in closer. "I really want to kiss you right now," he whispered.

"Please don't," she begged. "Not with everyone here." He grinned at her, and her heart pounded.

He turned to his workers. "Everyone make yourself a coffee." He turned back to her. "Thank you. This looks delicious."

He sat at the table and grabbed a slice of pound cake, then staring directly at her, licked his lips.

Was he trying to taunt her?

For the next few weeks Faith did her best to keep her distance from Jonah. It wasn't the easiest thing to do. Living in the same house made it excruciatingly difficult, but she vowed not to continue a relationship with him.

What would she do if things didn't work out between them? Not only would it affect Faith and the children, it would also affect Martha, who could no longer cope with either the children or the house on her own.

Whenever he moved close to her, she found a reason to move away. It was obvious he was confused at this sudden turnaround, but it was for the benefit of them both. She had become quite close to the twins, and despite their naughtiness at times, she knew she couldn't bear it if she had to leave. They'd become like her own children.

Martha had become like a mother-in-law.

The thought took her breath away. What would it be like to be married to Jonah?

Faith shook herself. The last thing she needed was to let her thoughts run away, to think about the man who was out of bounds.

At least to her.

The children were running around the house and going silly. She'd tried just about everything, but they wouldn't settle.

She stood in the middle of the sitting room, where they played. "I wonder if there are any children who would like to play outside for a little while? Hmmm." She looked around the room pretending they weren't there.

The pair ran toward her almost knocking her over, as they were apt to do.

"We do! We do, Faith!"

She glanced down at them and smiled. "You will need your warm coats and mittens. It's very cold outside."

Cora glanced up at her. "Papa said it might snow soon." Her little eyes opened wide with excitement.

"It will be Christmas soon," Leo added. "Papa told us." He clapped his little hands with joy. An action that was uniquely Leo when he was excited.

"Christmas is still a couple of weeks away," Faith told them quietly.

They pair ran toward their coats, and tried to pull them on. They pulled on their mittens, then reached for the door handle, which was too high for them. Thank goodness. Faith didn't want them running outside alone – there were far too many hazards on a ranch for small children.

She pulled on her own coat and gloves, and helped the children into theirs. Then they made their way down the porch steps. She'd barely been outside since she arrived, so this was to be an adventure for her as well.

"Let's go for a walk," she suggested as the twins pulled her toward the barn. "We can come back later and see the horses."

"Please, Faith," Leo begged, desperate to see the horses.

Cora had to get in on the act as well, of course. "Please?"

She was on the verge of giving in, when she remembered the words Martha had said. "You give in once, they'll expect it all the time."

They were mischievous children, especially when they were together, and had to be carefully controlled.

"We'll go for a walk first, then we'll see the horses," she said firmly. They both pouted but no longer argued.

They walked the perimeter of the house. Faith found a little vegetable garden around the side, but it had been badly neglected. She bent over and pulled out a few weeds. It already looked better. Weather permitting, she would spend time on this little vegetable patch. Perhaps when the children were sleeping.

It would only take a small amount of time each day to get it back to normal.

"Do you know what this is children?" She glanced across at them, but they just stared at her. "This is a vegetable patch. Look," She grabbed at some foliage and gently pulled. "This is where carrots come from. If I dig deep enough, I'll bet there are some potatoes in there."

She pulled off one glove and dug around. Sure enough, there were.

"What are you doing?" Jonah's voice startled her. He sounded annoyed.

Her head shot up. "We're checking out the vegetable garden. You didn't tell me it was here. I…"

"Leave it." He moved closer toward her, and Faith stepped back, her heart pounding, her shoulders stiff.

The children ran behind her.

She frowned. "Is something wrong, Jonah?"

He suddenly rubbed his grubby hands across his face. "I'm sorry," he said, clearly annoyed with himself. "It was my wife's vegetable garden. My mother was looking after it, but it got too much for her."

Now she was confused. "Well someone must be looking after it – we have vegetables in the pantry."

"I've been buying them from the greengrocer in town." He squatted down to the children's level and held his arms out to them. Did he even realize he'd scared them earlier?

"I won't touch it again," she said, feeling deflated at having to ignore such a wonderful source of fresh produce.

He glanced up at her and frowned, then stood with the children in his arms. "I'm being stupid. And ridiculous," he said. "You are welcome to do whatever you want with it." He smiled tentatively, and she felt his pain.

"Papa," Cora said, touching her fingers to Jonah's cheek as she always did when she wanted his attention. "We're going to visit the horses."

He frowned, then glanced at Faith. "Can Papa come too?"

Did he not trust her to keep the children safe? "I am capable of looking after them you know," she said. She knew she sounded annoyed, and he must had heard it in her voice because his head shot up.

"I know," he said gently. "I thought they might like to ride one of the horses."

She jerked her head. "Of course. I can't do that."

He moved closer to her. "No, you can't. Faith," he said quietly as he put the children back on the ground. "Do we have a problem? You seem to be avoiding me."

She stepped away. "No, not at all." It was a lie and she knew it. It had proved incredibly difficult to keep away from him. All she wanted him to do right now was put his arms around her and hold her tight.

"Have I offended you in some way?" His gaze was intense, and she couldn't look away.

"It's nothing like that," she said, then tore her gaze away and stared at the ground.

"Uh huh." He didn't sound as though he believed her.

The twins pulled at his breeches. "When are we going to ride the horse, Papa?" He stared down at them.

"In a minute. Can you wait for just a minute?"

"Papa," they said, their tone disappointed.

He stared at her for long moments, then glanced down at his children. "Right. Let's go," he said, as he picked them up and headed toward the barn.

"Are you coming?" he asked Faith as she stood staring after them, her heart shattering into a million pieces, as it had every time she'd stood firm on her decision to keep her distance from him.

Chapter Eight

Faith held the hands of the children while Jonah retrieved all the equipment he would need for the children to ride.

They then went out to the front paddock where the horses ran free. He climbed through the fence, and coaxed Maisy. She was the quietest of all the horses they had on the ranch, and had always been earmarked for the children to ride. Besides, she was the smallest.

"You can only ride one at a time," Jonah said firmly, already believing this was a bad idea, despite it being his own.

"But Papa…"

He stared at them. "One at a time or not at all." He finished fastening the saddle, and checked the reins. It was a long way down if everything was not secure. He reached over and grabbed Cora. "You're first."

Her grin was so wide he thought it would split her face. "I'll be standing right next to you." He held her hands in his. "Hold the rein, like this," he said, showing her how. "Now we'll go for a short walk."

Cora squealed as they began to slowly move around the paddock. "You need to stop squealing or you have to get off. You'll scare the horse." Maisy was old and placid. Despite what he said, Jonah knew she wouldn't even flinch.

When they returned she had tears running down her little face. He leaned over to Faith and whispered conspiratorially. "She's a bit over excited, I think."

"You think?" she said, a scowl on her face. She cuddled into Cora, trying to calm her down.

"Leo's turn now." He swung the child up into the saddle and began to move around the same area. At least he didn't squeal like his sister.

"This is fun, Papa," Leo said.

"It can be," Jonah told him. Perhaps when he was older Leo would want to help out on the ranch. But that was a very long while off yet.

When the ride ended, Jonah swung him down to the ground and returned him to Faith. "It's nearly time for their nap," she said. "I'm not sure they'll be able to sleep after this."

"Sorry," he whispered. It was the first time they'd done an activity together like this, and it almost felt like they were a family. They had already begun to feel like a family when she'd suddenly pulled back from him.

A thought suddenly hit him – were the two things related?

"They can play quietly in their rooms, I guess," she said, gazing into his eyes. She suddenly pulled them away. "Let's go children."

They both complained loudly.

Jonah stared after them until they nearly reached the house, then sprinted toward them. It was the perfect time to talk to Faith; the children would be in their rooms, and the adults would finally be alone. Ma was visiting a friend, so the house was otherwise empty.

"Faith," he called after her, and she spun around.

"I have to organize the children," she said, ushering them inside, out of the cold.

He motioned for her to continue.

Jonah helped Leo out of his coat and Faith did the same for Cora. They were a good team.

"Go and wash your hands and I'll organize a snack before you have your nap."

He groaned inwardly. How long before they'd be alone?

"Would you like a coffee?" she asked him.

Not really. He only wanted to talk, but if it meant he would get physically close to her… "Thank you, yes." He took a few steps toward her. "I can get it myself. You have enough to do."

She ignored his comment and pulled a mug from the cupboard anyway. She put some milk on the table for each of the twins, as well as an oat cookie each. They came scrambling out of the bathroom and bounded up onto the kitchen chairs.

"Cookies!"

"They are overwrought after their ride," she told him quietly, and he felt guilty for being the cause of the problem.

She sat a mug of coffee on the table and he sat down opposite his children, watching them carefully. Assessing the way they reacted to Faith. She was like a mother to them.

"Have a cookie," she said quietly, and he reached out, not to grab a cookie from the plate, but to touch her. He'd missed that so much, but she'd kept her distance and it had nearly killed him. He had to find out what he'd done to cause all this.

The contact with her skin caused electricity to run up his arm. It zinged around his body and exploded in his heart. He stared at her. She quickly pulled her hand back and he knew she'd felt it too.

"What are we doing?" he asked her quietly. "We both know this is not what we want."

"I'm tired," Cora said, as she yawned.

Leo yawned as well. "Me too."

They both climbed down from the table and took themselves off to bed.

"I, I need to get them tucked in," Faith said, and he nodded. She had to do what she had to do. Besides, they might finally get the privacy they needed.

He drank his coffee and ate his cookie, but he was only going through the motions. Just as he'd been doing since Faith had made it clear she wanted nothing more to do with him.

His work had suffered, and he'd barely been able to sleep. Something had to change, and soon.

When she returned, she refused to look at him. She made herself a cup of tea and sat at the table opposite him after cleaning up after the children.

"Do you ever stop?" he asked gruffly. "I need to talk to you."

She stared at him, and her expression told him she was afraid of what he was going to say. "I, I can be gone tomorrow," she said, tears in her eyes.

"What?" He stood abruptly. "No, that's not what I want. Let's go and sit by the fire." He'd managed to get her to open up there in the past. Perhaps she would again? She'd distanced herself from him so much that he honestly didn't know anymore.

Jonah sat on the sofa and Faith sat opposite. His heart pounded. The last thing he wanted was to drive her away. He couldn't bear if she left them, and he knew the children felt the same way. They were young enough to get over it, but his heart would never be the same again.

No matter what, they couldn't continue the way things were now.

It had been difficult for him to come to terms with his feelings, there was no doubt. He had loved Sarah immensely and thought he'd never love again. Then along came Faith. Beautiful, vulnerable Faith who stole his heart far too quickly.

"Faith," he said quietly, balancing on the edge of the sofa. She stared into the fire and refused to look at him. "Please, look at me."

She turned her head toward him and glanced in his direction, but didn't say a word. He could tell she was upset, but for some crazy reason, she thought he was sending her away.

"Do you like it here on the ranch?"

She nodded.

"Do you like working with the children?"

She nodded again.

He stared at her, studied her face now that the bruising had finally cleared. "Do you want to stay here?" He swallowed hard. His heart beat roared in his head as he waited for her answer.

She nodded again.

"Oh for goodness sakes," he said quietly. "Can you please speak to me? You're breaking my heart here." He leaned back on the sofa and stared intently at her. Why wouldn't she give anything away? Tell him how she felt. She'd said not a single word since they'd moved to the sitting room.

"I don't want to leave," she said softly, and he watched as she blinked the tears back. He reached out and took both her hands. It was the first time he'd held her hands in two weeks. That's how long it had been since she'd driven a wedge between them, but it felt like two years.

"What do you want, Faith?" The words came out on a sigh, and he wished he could say them again, this time more compassionately. It was obvious she was hurting, but the reason was totally unknown to him. And it stung.

She glanced down into her lap, and he was afraid he'd never find out what the problem was. He couldn't continue like this. He couldn't live under the same roof as Faith and not touch her, not hold her. Not comfort her.

His heart ached.

"I can't have what I want," she said, her voice barely above a whisper. Was her heart breaking too, only over something else? Or worse still, someone else?

Still holding her hands, he stood, bringing her up with him. She glanced up at him, her sad brown eyes breaking his heart all over again.

He swallowed hard. "What is it you want, Faith?" His head was spinning, and his heart had shattered.

She took a step back. Her voice broke as she said the words. "You. I want you." Her tears overflowed and he pulled her close, wrapping his arms around her.

How could he have been so stupid? They'd already wasted far too much time. It had to end now. "I want you too," he said gently. "I have loved you almost from the moment you arrived." He lifted her chin gently and kissed her.

"I love you too," she said, then relaxed into him. He lost count of how long they'd stood there entwined in each other. "Marry me?" She stepped back, and he saw the surprise on her face. "We can get married Saturday if you say yes."

Her hand lifted and caressed his unshaven face. "Yes," she said. "I will marry you."

"Finally," Martha said as she flung open the door. "Does this mean I can finally go back home?"

The wedding was a small affair, and was exactly what they both wanted.

The twins were there of course, and carried the wedding rings. How safe that would be was yet to be proven.

Hank and Martha were the witnesses, and Percy and Rory came for the ceremony too. With her permission, Jonah had contacted her father, Harry.

He'd told Jonah he regretted his behavior, and since Faith had left home, both he and Martin had stopped drinking. He knew it was already too late by the time he realized what he had really lost – the love and respect of his only daughter.

He'd worn his best suit today, and cleaned himself up. She almost didn't recognize him. As they stood at the entrance to the Mountain Ridge church, nestled in the town named after the ranch, he embraced his daughter. "I'm sorry, Faith," he said quietly. "I was devastated over your mother's death, but that's no excuse."

She swallowed back the emotion that threatened to take over. Under no circumstances would Faith stand next to her soon-to-be husband with red puffy eyes.

She hooked her arm through Harry's and they slowly walked down the aisle to the organ music.

Martha had taken her into town a few days ago, and they'd chosen a new gown for Faith to wear for her wedding. It was the most beautiful gown she'd ever seen. She glanced down at it as they moved toward her soon-to-be husband, and a smile crossed her face. No matter what she'd worn, Jonah would think her beautiful anyway. He'd told her so many times now.

Harry presented her to Jonah, and she noticed tears in his eyes. She had forgiven him and Martin, and hoped they could have a better, closer relationship now.

Jonah took her hands and encased them in his, then they turned to face the preacher. The same preacher who had helped Jonah through his wife's death.

"Dearly Beloved," Preacher Dean said, looking out at those sitting in the pews. "We have come together today to join this man and this woman in holy matrimony."

The twins stood next to their father while the ceremony took place. Leo tugged at his father's breeches. "What does that mean?" he asked loudly. Everyone chuckled.

"You may kiss your bride," Preacher Dean announced once he'd pronounced them man and wife, and that's exactly what Jonah did. Faith wasn't sure he would ever let her come up for air.

They turned to leave the church, and Martha came up to them both and hugged them tight. "Welcome to the family, Faith," she said with tears in her eyes. "You have made my son very happy." She brushed her tears aside. "I'm very happy too."

The new couple each clutched the hand of one of the twins and they left the church. Once outside, Harry came up to them and stood in front of Faith and stared. It was as though he was frozen to the spot. Martin joined him and hugged his sister. "I'm really sorry, Sis," he said. "I promise it won't happen again.

When he stepped back, Harry finally moved in. Faith thought he would never let her go. It would take a long time for their relationship to fully mend, but this was a good first step.

Cora tugged on Harry's breeches. "Who are you," she asked, staring up at him.

He glanced down at her. "I'm your grandpa," he said with tears in his eyes.

A week later it was Christmas, and Faith had put together a family gathering for Christmas Day.

Harry and Martin had been invited to stay on after the wedding, and had accepted the invitation. Jonah wanted Faith to be able to spend time with her family and hopefully mend some of those broken ties, and build trust between them again.

The twins had taken to their new grandpa and uncle, both who realized if they went backwards with their drinking, they would be banished from Faith's life forever. She'd told them in no uncertain terms.

Jonah didn't blame her one little bit.

He glanced around the table. Everyone he loved and cared about was there, as well as the two he was only beginning to get to know. Hank, Percy, and Rory were ecstatic. They'd never had such an elaborate Christmas dinner.

Faith had prepared most of the food herself, with a little help from Martha who was happy to be able to step back for once. Harry and Martin sat wide-eyed at the array of food, as much as the twins did. They were on their best behavior. Faith had done wonders with them from the moment she'd arrived.

If someone had told Jonah he'd be this happy, he wouldn't have believed them. Sarah would never be forgotten, but Faith had filled a gaping hole in his heart, and for that he would be forever grateful.

He glanced across at the Christmas tree in the corner near the fireplace. Martin helped him find the tree and cut it down, and everyone had helped decorate it. The twins had even made some paper chains for it, with a lot of help.

Faith pulled the last of the roasted vegetables from the oven and added them to the platter. Jonah couldn't help himself, he put his arms around her and held her close. "I love you so much," he said so only Faith could hear.

"I love you too," she said, then got up onto her tiptoes and kissed him.

This was a Christmas he would never forget.

Epilogue

Almost One Year Later…

Faith couldn't believe it had been a little over a year since she and Jonah had married. Things had only got better since then.

Martin had come to work for Jonah on the ranch, and turned out to be a really good worker. With the help of Hank and the other workers, they'd built a small cottage not far from the bunkhouse so Harry could stay nearby. Like the workers, he had his meals in the main house, and spent evenings with them. If he wanted privacy, he only needed to walk a short distance and he was home.

The twins enjoyed having their grandpa living close by. They were still pranksters, but had calmed down considerably.

The fire burned brightly and Faith pulled her shawl up around her shoulders and sat down. Martin and Jonah had taken the twins to cut down a tree for Christmas. The children were beyond excited and spent most of the week making decorations, with a little help.

Three days until Christmas, and she'd been baking furiously in preparation for Christmas Day. Perhaps that's why she felt so tired all of a sudden? Faith swiveled on the sofa and lay her head against the cushion. She couldn't keep her eyes open.

"Mama! Mama!" Little voices startled her awake. "It's snowing! Come and see."

Martin and Jonah carried the tree into the sitting room. "You found a tree," Faith said, still half asleep. She stood and lost her balance. Jonah reached out and steadied her.

"Are you alright," he asked as he held her.

She glanced up at him. "I'm just tired. I'll be fine." She turned to the twins. "Show me the snow," and the three of them went outside together.

She stood on the porch and glanced about. There wasn't much but it was beautiful to look at. It wouldn't be long and it would be quite thick and the children would be begging to build a snowman.

Cora shouted as she rubbed her hand against Faith's protruding belly. "Papa! Papa! Mama has wet herself!"

Faith looked down. No wonder she was feeling so tired – the baby was coming. Jonah rushed outside, concern etched on his face.

She glanced across at him. "Sorry," she said. "I didn't realize until it was too late."

He swooped in and picked her up, carrying Faith into the bedroom. "Martin," he said as he carried her. "We'll need the doctor. Have Hank run into town, will you?"

"Is Mama sick?" Cora asked, tears running down her little cheeks.

"No silly," Leo told her. "Papa just likes carrying her."

Faith glanced up to see a smile on Jonah's face despite the distress he was under over the situation. Her laid her gently on the bed, and the twins came in to check on her. "Are you sick, Mama," Cora asked, her tears still flowing.

"No sweetheart," Faith told her gently, wiping her tears away. "Our new baby is ready to arrive."

Two pairs of eyes opened wide, then they hugged each other. "We're getting a baby," they sang and jumped up and down as they chanted.

"Right you two," Jonah said firmly. "You need to go out and let Mama rest. Uncle Martin will take care of you." Martin came in and took each of their hands.

"Love you, Sis," he said before he left the room with the over excited twins.

Faith closed her eyes and rested until she could rest no more.

By the time Doc Henderson arrived, Faith was having strong contractions. Jonah had sat by her side the whole time, holding her hands. He felt useless and helpless, but Martha had told him there wasn't much else he could do.

Once the doc had set himself up, much to his disgust, Jonah had been sent away.

When the screams began, the children were distraught so he put their coats and mittens on them, and they went outside.

"I wonder if there's enough snow to build a snowman?" He was trying to distract them, and it worked. They ran outside and off the porch, waiting at the bottom of the steps.

Harry was standing outside his cottage, and came over to see them. "What's going on?" he asked curiously.

"We're going to build a snowman," Leo told him seriously.

"The baby is coming," Jonah told him quietly.

Harry grinned, then looked to the ground. "I doubt that very much," he told Leo. "Perhaps in a few days there might be enough snow. Why don't you visit Maisy instead?"

Jonah sighed with relief. "That's a good idea, Grandpa."

The twins were good riders now, but were never left alone. They were far too little. Jonah let them ride Maisy in the large barn out of the weather.

After what seemed like hours, he glanced up to see Martha standing on the porch waving him in.

"You go," Harry said. "I'll look after the twins and sort out Maisy."

He didn't say no to the offer – Harry knew what he was doing. Jonah near ran to the house. "It's a boy," Martha said, tears brimming in her eyes. They hugged, then he quickly went to his wife.

She lay dozing on the bed, the baby in her arms. "Congratulations," Doc Henderson told him. "You have a healthy boy. Faith is fine too," he said, preempting Jonah's question.

"Thanks Doc," Jonah said. He sat on the edge of the bed and glanced down at his wife and new son. He leaned in and kissed Faith on the forehead and she glanced up at him. "I love you," he told her quietly.

"I love you too," she said.

The twins came running in, their excitement running over. "You have a baby brother," Jonah said, and held the baby out for them to see.

They stared at the baby then at each other, and hugged each other tight. "We have a baby," Leo said matter-of-factly.

"I know," Cora said, then burst into tears.

Jonah silently prayed his thanks for his beautiful family, and also for bringing Faith to him. He knew this wouldn't be their last addition, there was so much love in their home, it was inevitable.

The twins interrupted his thoughts as they ran over to the window. "Papa, look!" Cora shouted.

"Lots of snow," Leo said. "Can we go and make a snowman now?"

Jonah glanced around the room. Love filled his heart like it had never been filled before.

From the Author

Thank you so much for reading my book – I hope you enjoyed it.

I would greatly appreciate you leaving a review where you purchased, even if it is only a one-liner. It helps to have my books more visible!

About the Author

Multi-published, award-winning and bestselling author Cheryl Wright, former secretary, debt collector, account manager, writing coach, and shopping tour hostess, loves reading.

She writes historical romantic suspense and historical western romance.

She lives in Melbourne, Australia, and is married with two adult children and has six grandchildren, and twin great-grandchildren.

When she's not writing, she can be found in her craft room making greeting cards.

Links

Website: *http://www.cheryl-wright.com/*

Facebook Reader Group:
https://www.facebook.com/groups/cherylwrightaut hor/

Join My Newsletter:

https://cheryl-wright.com/newsletter/
(and receive a free book)

www.ingramcontent.com/pod-product-compliance
Lightning Source LLC
Chambersburg PA
CBHW070406200726

48294CB00003B/1123